The Legend of the Peacock Throne

Theresa Edwards

Cover Illustration by Miné Jonker

DEDICATION

To my husband and my children who provide me with such joy!

CHAPTER ONE

Julia ran up to her mother with that special glint in her eyes,

'Mum, what are we doing for the July holidays?'

Mrs McKenzie knew exactly what would follow and turned to her with a little smile, 'Why, Julia, are you planning anything?'

'Well, Jessica just Sms'd me to find out what we will be doing,' replied Julia.

Trying hard to hide her laughter, Mrs McKenzie looked at her daughter and asked, 'Well, what are you doing? You know your dad will be working and your sister and I thought you would like to spend some special time with us these holidays, as we don't get to see you much because of boarding school.'

At that Julia looked a bit worried, 'Ah Mum, you see me every weekend, it's not as if I only come home at term end! Anyhow, Morag and I spend every weekend playing together.'

Her mother hid another small smile as she teased, 'But you know your sister loves you to bits and loves playing with her big sister.' Then suppressing yet another grin she added, 'It's not every day a ten-year old has a six-month-old playmate; think of it as having a real, live doll.'

By this stage Julia was becoming extremely agitated; she had to think fast and very hard for a really good reply. 'Yes, I know she loves to play with me mum, but she also sleeps a lot and then I'm bored with nothing to do!'

'Oh,' said Mrs McKenzie, 'you get bored do you? Well, there are lots of things you could help me with you know!'

Julia gulped and rushed on, knowing she had not answered correctly, 'But Mum, I don't mean I get bored with helping you, I just...' Thinking hard again, because she knew how important it would be to get this answer perfect, she said, 'I just need to play with friends my own age, Mum! We live far away from them and that's why I get bored!'

'Oh right,' said her mother, 'because we live on a farm, far away from other children, you get bored!

Most children would love to live on a farm with live animals, their own horse, dogs, tractors to ride on and their own quad bike!' She was now openly smiling as she teased Julia who was looking decidedly worried.

'You may as well tell me now, my girl,' she continued, 'what have you three monkeys planned this time? The last time you and your cousins got together, it involved all sorts of shenanigans and, if I remember correctly, you, Jessica and Jarred were in real danger at one stage!'

She became very serious for a moment and thought back to the previous holidays and the adventure the three cousins had had together. She shook her shoulders to forget the memories and looked at Julia with a proud glance. Her young daughter was growing up so fast. In fact, all three cousins were such close friends and it made her so proud to have such a family.

Jessica lived in Mozambique. They all called her the 'little American' because she attended an American School in Maputo and over the years had picked up an American accent. She was a whiz at computers, very intelligent, but a bit impulsive at times.

Then there was little Jarred who lived with his mother in Cape Town, a real little boy in all respects, constantly up to mischief at every turn.

Finally, there was Julia, or Jules as her mother sometimes affectionately called her, a real farm girl, tall, athletic and brilliant at horse riding and sports, although a little help in the classroom would not go amiss.

By this stage Julia was jumping up and down on one leg, 'Mum! July remember!'

'First show me Jessica's SMS so that I can see what you chaps have planned!'

Julia ran to fetch her cellphone and her mother read the following cryptic message on the screen: July! Remember. Berg or C? U 2 choose!

'Right, Julia, best you explain this to me,' said her mother, looking perplexed.

'All right, Mum. Last holiday Jessica, Jarred and I made a pact that we would spend every July holiday together, forever!' said Julia, looking very proud of herself.

'Oh you did, did you?' remarked Mrs McKenzie, permitting herself a little giggle on the side. 'And when were the three of you going to inform us, the mums and dads?'

'Well, we just thought it would be fine,' said Julia. 'You know we never see each other, other than holidays, and we thought the parents would agree.

We live in KwaZulu-Natal, Jarred is in Cape Town and Jessica is far away in Mozambique.'

Julia's confidence had returned and she was bubbling with excitement. She knew she was right and was sure that her mother could not resist this answer.

Mrs McKenzie looked a bit pensive for a moment. 'Yes, it's awful that we all live so far away and only see one another from time to time. I really miss my brothers and sister and look forward to seeing them.'

Julia jumped up and down with excitement. 'This is perfect, Mum! This way you can see your family every July.'

'Wait a minute, Julia, before you get too excited. Let me talk to Uncle Paul and Aunty Sylvia to find out from them first what plans they have made.'

'But, Mum,' said Julia with a huge smile, 'that's what the SMS means. Uncle Paul has given us a choice, either the mountains or the sea!'

'What do you mean, Julia?' questioned her mother, now looking totally confused.

'Uncle Paul has arranged our holiday.'

'When did this happen?' Mrs McKenzie asked, quite intrigued. Julia beamed, 'Last year. I told you we made a pact that we would spend every July holiday together. Well, Uncle Paul made us sign this pact in blood!'

Her mother looked horrified. 'What do you mean, Julia? Sign this pact in blood! What blood?'

Julia screamed with laughter. 'Not real blood, Mum, fake blood! We squeezed some juice out of a beetroot plant and all signed our names in blood. Beetroot blood!'

'Let me get this straight, Julia. When you went to Mozambique last July for your holiday, you, Jessica and Jarred all signed a pact with the help of your uncle, my brother, in blood! Fake blood. Why didn't anyone tell me this?'

'That's the point. Uncle Paul said we must keep it a secret as all pacts signed in blood are a secret, Mum, you know that,' said Julia, very pleased with herself.

'Hmm,' said her mother, 'now my brother is conspiring against me to keep you cousins entertained. But I should have known better than to send you to Mozambique and have Uncle Paul look after you. He is such a trickster at times.'

'But, Mum, he is so much fun! And he is so funny, he makes us laugh all the time.'

'Yeah,' agreed Mrs McKenzie, smiling fondly, 'he really is a card sometimes. I don't know how Aunty Jeannie keeps up with him. However, when we were children, he was always so serious and responsible. He was like another father to us, especially when my mum, Granny Anne, passed away. Your besta fa (Norwegian for 'grandfather') had to go back to sea – he was a ship's captain – soon after, and because Aunty Sylvia had already left home, Uncle Paul took over the running of the family. That was an enormous amount of responsibility for a 20-year old. Your Uncle John was only 15 and I was only 17 at the time. Uncle Paul is a very special person in our lives. That's why it's lovely to see him like this now, full of fun and getting on so well with you children.

He is my best friend, you know.'

Julia looked at her mother. She knew how much she missed her family and was often sad that she could not spend more time with them.

'Right, Julia, that's enough reminiscing so let's get back to the reason for this conversation. What has Uncle Paul arranged? Details please????'

Julia smiled widely as she knew she had won the day! She was going on holiday.

'Well, Uncle Paul has given us a choice: we can either go to this lovely holiday camp in the Drakensberg or a super one at Umhlali on the North Coast. Jessica sent me an e-mail to school, giving me the website and it looks really cool, Mum.

'At the Berg there are hikes we can go on. We can ride horses, abseil, go on nature trails or we can choose the beach option and learn to surf, collect shells or swim in the ocean. They both look like so much fun!' Julia was becoming really excited and was starting to babble.

'Slow down, Jules,' said her mother. 'Let me e-mail Uncle Paul and find out where he thinks would be best for the three of you. I also need to find out how much this is going to cost us. Don't forget that we are just farmers and we need to budget for these types of things.'

Julia's face fell for a second as she saw her dream holiday flying out the window and Mrs McKenzie's heart went out to her.

'Don't worry, my girl, I have a little money put aside, but we will have to be careful and make sure we are getting a good deal from the holiday camp.'

Visibly relieved, Julia said, 'Don't worry about spending money, Mum, I have saved my allowance for the whole year so that I could help out when it was holiday time.'

'Good girl, Julia, I am very proud of you. You are showing that you can also be responsible.'

CHAPTER TWO

In tears, Julia ran to her mother and held out a sheet of paper.

'Julia,' exclaimed Mrs McKenzie, 'what's wrong?'

'Mum, I have the worst news ever. I just received an e-mail from Jarred and he can't come!'

'What do you mean "can't come"? I thought all three of you had this pact where you would spend every July holiday together.'

'Yes I know, but Aunty Sylvia said she can't afford this holiday and now Jarred can't come!' cried Julia, sobbing her heart out.

Her heart breaking, Julia's mother looked at her daughter and said, 'Come here, Jules, don't worry, leave this to me and we will try to sort something out.'

Mrs McKenzie went to her office on the farm and placed a call to Jarred's mother in Cape Town. 'Hi, Sylvia, how are you?'

'Hey, Anne, I'm fine and I know precisely why you are calling. I have a ten-year old who has locked himself up in his room for the last four hours and I just don't know what to do.'

'Are you battling with costs, Sylvia?' asked Julia's mother.

'Yes, I am. Jarred's father never pays the maintenance on time and we are having a bad time at the moment, I simply can't afford this holiday. I feel terrible for Jarred, but I really don't have too many options,' explained Aunty Sylvia.

'Well, let's put our heads together. Surely we can come up with a plan,' said Mrs McKenzie to her sister.

'I've been racking my brains for days,' Jarred's mother said wearily, 'and I don't know what to do. It's so unfair that Jarred has to suffer because his father refuses to pay.'

'Yes, it is sad, Sylvia, but let's not discard the idea. I am sure we can think of a solution. I'll make a couple of calls and see what I can do,' promised Mrs McKenzie.

Julia looked at her mother, knowing what would happen next. She left the office to give her a little privacy for that all-important phone call and even felt some pity for Jarred's father because she knew how fierce her mother could be when someone was hurt.

Mum always helped the farm staff to sort out their problems and sometimes even took the government to task over injustices.

Once, when 45 children did not attend school because their parents couldn't afford the fees, Julia remembered how her mother contacted everyone in government she could think of, until she spoke to the Director of Education in Ulundi himself.

He personally flew down to their town and discovered that the school principal had illegally suspended the children. He was severely reprimanded and the children were accepted back at school. Her mum received a note of thanks from the government for fighting for these children's right to receive an education.

'Hello Bert, how are you?' enquired Mrs McKenzie.

Bert (Jarred's father), somewhat taken aback when he heard her voice said guardedly, 'I am fine, Anne, how are you?'

'This is not a social call, Bert. I'm calling because Jarred is sitting in Cape Town in an awful state.'

'Why, what's wrong?' asked his father, alarmed.

'Well,' said Anne McKenzie, 'it appears you have not been playing ball and your son is suffering the consequences.'

Bert, realizing what she meant, became defensive, 'This has nothing to do with you, Anne!'

'Yes, Bert, I agree to a certain extent, but when a little boy's happiness is jeopardized by your selfishness, it becomes my business,' she shot back.

'Well,' said Bert, 'what can I do?'

'Firstly, you can pay the maintenance you owe. Then I need you to deposit another R800 into my account for Jarred's July holiday.'

'R800!' exclaimed Bert. 'What for?'

'Jarred, Julia and Jessica are going on an adventure camp and I need to book his place for the July holiday,' said Julia's mum.

'That's a lot of money and I don't think he needs to go on an adventure camp,' said Bert smugly.

'Well, Bert, if you recall, last year Jarred went to Mozambique on holiday. Who paid for that? And for Christmas last year, Jarred came to the farm. Who paid for that?'

A little embarrassed, Bert acknowledged, 'You did, Anne.'

'Well, Bert, this time I'm not paying, you are.'

'You can't force me,' he said.

'You're right, I can't, Bert, but what I can do is drive down to Pietermaritzburg and sit in your office and tell everyone and anyone who will listen that you "forget" to pay maintenance on a monthly basis and the last time you saw your son was over a year ago. I can also tell them Jarred needs new school shoes, some additional clothes, and much more.'

'Ok! Ok!' Bert said hurriedly, 'I get the point. This is bribery, Anne, but I know you well. You'd come to my office, wouldn't you?'

'Yes I would. I cannot accept it that children must suffer for the mistakes of their parents! Please deposit the money into my account before Friday and don't forget to catch up with your maintenance as well,' she added with a satisfied smile.

'Hello, Anne,' said Jarred's mum. 'What did you do? I have just come from the bank and there is money in my account. It's like Christmas! How did you persuade Bert to pay up?'

Mrs McKenzie simply smiled and said, 'Bribery, I think Bert called it! I also have R800 in my bank account. Tell Jarred he is coming on holiday.'

CHAPTER THREE

'Dad, should I take this T shirt with me?' asked Jessica, holding up the umpteenth garment.

Her father looked up from his book and smiled patiently, 'Take whatever you think you will need for your holiday, Jessica.'

'Do you think it will be cold in the Berg, Dad?' she continued.

'Yes,' he said, 'it's normally very hot during the day, but very cold at night – after all, it's July and the middle of winter. So don't forget to pack for both cold and warm weather.'

'Oh, it's going to be such fun,' said Jessica, jumping excitedly around the room. 'Jarred flies in from Cape Town on Tuesday and Aunty Anne will collect me on Wednesday from the airport. How far is the Berg from Durban, Dad?'

'Well,' said her father, smiling, 'it's about a three-hour drive from Durban. If you're lucky, you might even see snow on the mountains whilst you're there. The snow we experience in South Africa is much wetter than the dry snow they have overseas.'

'Snow,' squealed Jessica, 'maybe we can have real snowball fights and make angels, as we did the year we went to Norway!'

'Yes, but it won't be quite as thick as we had on holiday in Norway,' said her father.

Jessica smiled and jumped up to hug him. 'Dad, you are the "bestest" dad in the world! We've had so many lovely holidays overseas – Norway, England, France and America.'

'My girl, I suppose it helps that I work for an overseas company. Your mum and I also felt you should see where your Fa fa (their grandfather's nickname) came from in Norway and that you should meet your family over there.

'Yes,' she agreed, 'I just love my Norwegian family. They are all so big and tall – Gunnar is like a mountain, Dad!'

Her father laughed, 'Don't forget how big Fa fa was, Jessica. He was well over 2 m tall, while his own father, my grandfather, was even taller!'

'Are all Norwegians tall, Dad?'

'They mostly are all tall. Look how tall you are – at ten you're already towering over your friends. And even little Morag at six months already looks as though she is ten months old! It obviously skipped a generation with Aunty Anne, Uncle John and myself, but is coming out in the grandchildren – you and Morag,' said her father.

'But then I don't understand. Why are Julia and Jarred not as tall as we are?'

Jessica's father thought a while before taking a deep breath. 'I'm sure you remember what we explained to you about Julia's story, don't you?

Soon after she was born, she was abandoned, which means that her biological or real mother disappeared without ever going back to collect her from the place she had left her.

In the meanwhile, Aunty Anne, who was not married at the time, had applied to the welfare department to adopt a black baby.'
Jessica looked at her father with wide eyes, 'Why did Aunty Anne want to adopt a black baby and not a white one, Dad?'
'Well,' he began, 'when Aunty Anne considered her options, she decided that as she lived in a rural community, she would be able to give a black child the benefit of two worlds, the understanding of city life (from her own experience) as well as the freedom and fun of living in a country environment that hasn't lost all the important traditions of African heritage and culture.
'Initially she was told she wouldn't be allowed to adopt, because that would make her a single mother, but you know your Aunty Anne! She doesn't take no for an answer. She fought the system and eventually the welfare department decided to use her as a test case and she became the first white, single (unmarried), South African woman to foster and then adopt a black baby.
'If only more people would consider doing what she did, there wouldn't be so many poor, little ones left in orphanages in South Africa. Aunty Anne got Julia when she was only two weeks' old.

Then, of course, when Julia was six months' old Aunty Anne met Uncle George and the rest is history.

'So Julia is not Aunty Anne's biological child, but her adopted child. Aunty Anne has a lovely expression for this – she tells Julia she is not her tummy baby but her heart baby! She comes from the love in her heart.

'Now remember also that Aunty Anne was told she would never be able to have her own children because she was infertile. This meant she could not conceive a child, but then you also know Aunty Anne had Morag in April. She is our family's miracle baby! Suddenly, after 20 years of not being able to have a child, your Aunty Anne fell pregnant and had Morag. The doctors cannot explain why but I believe it was a gift sent to her from God.'

'That's one reason why we love Aunty Anne so much, isn't it, Dad?' said Jessica. 'But what about Jarred?

Why isn't he tall like me and Morag?'

'Morag and I!' corrected her father. 'Well, that is another story. My mum, Granny Anne, also battled to have children, then after trying for so many years, Fa fa and Granny Anne decided to adopt a child. They adopted Aunty Sylvia when she was just three weeks' old. Later, through medical technology, granny Anne was able to conceive and carry her own children.

She had me first, Aunty Anne second, then your Uncle John. So, in effect, because Aunty Sylvia is also not my biological sister she doesn't have the "tall" genes we carry.'

Jessica thought about this for a while, then said, 'So although Julia and Aunty Sylvia are adopted, there is no real difference between being adopted and having your own children. We all love each other just as much as if they were not adopted. In the same way that Julia loves her stepbrother Greg and thinks of him as though he was her real brother.'

'Yes, Jessica,' said her father, 'you are so right. Granny Anne made sure we, as children, understood that we are all very special in our own way and love each other equally.'

'Thanks, Dad, for explaining that to me. Now I understand why we are all so special. Let me call Mum to help me pack the rest of my clothes.'

'Jessica, before you go I have something for you to take along on your trip,' said her father. He went to his desk and took out a small leather case. Jessica's eyes grew wide with excitement and surprise.

'Dad, that is your satellite cell with internet!' she exclaimed.

'Yes it is,' he said rather seriously.

'I know this is an expensive piece of equipment, but I also know you are responsible enough to look after it and that you know exactly how to use it. In light of the fact that you and your cousins are always on the lookout for adventure and remembering what happened the last time you got together, I would like you to take this with you so that you can be in constant contact with us anytime you may need it.

I want you to promise me that, should anything happen and you need our help, you will contact either me or Aunty Anne immediately.

I don't have to remind you that we will be there.'
Jessica took the leather pouch reverently and hugged her father. 'I promise, Dad, I will.'

4 CHAPTER FOUR

The sun was barely peaking its glorious, warm face over the low hills to the east and the birds had just begun their morning song, when three excited faces peered through the window overlooking the magnificent view of the mist- covered Drakensberg.

'Pinch me,' said Jarred. 'I can't believe we're eventually here.

Julia giggled and gave her cousin a huge pinch.

'Julia!' shouted Jarred. 'I didn't mean it that was sore.'

Jessica ran to the bed and jumped on it, bouncing up and down whilst screaming with laughter. 'We are here chaps, best you believe it.'

Jarred walked over slowly, still rubbing his arm. 'Yes we are here, what shall we do today?'

Julia looked quizzically at the other two and said, 'What do you mean, "what shall we do"? Do the camp team leaders not have everything planned for us?'

'Yeah right,' said Jarred, 'boring, boring, boring. Let's explore before everyone wakes up.'

The three cousins quickly pulled on their jerseys and jackets, because it was bitterly cold outside with the frost on the ground, the sun just peeking over the horizon. They crept outside and started to look around. The camp was situated at the foothills of the Drakensberg.

Julia looked at the other two and asked, 'Do you two know the fantastic history of the KwaZulu-Natal Drakensberg?'

Jarred and Jessica laughed and Jessica said, 'No, Julia, but I'm sure you are going to tell us… let's sit here awhile under this tree and tell us all.' She smiled at her cousin fondly, as it was a known fact that Julia's father was always teaching his children – and anyone else who would listen – fascinating facts about South Africa, the two World Wars and anything to do with history.

He was an absolute mine of information, much of which he had passed on to Julia. The children sat down under the tree and Julia started her recital.

'The KwaZulu-Natal Drakensberg, which now even contains its own World Heritage Site, was formed about 150 million years ago. The Zulu people called it uKhahlamba, which means Barrier of Spears, and it became the western boundary of their Zulu Kingdom.

'The ox-wagons of Boer voortrekkers struggled up its high, cliff passes in 1837 on the Great Trek from the Cape Colony, while they searched for their "Promised Land" to the east. The name "Drakensberg", which means "dragon mountain", was given 40 years later when a Boer father and his son reported seeing a dragon – a giant lizard with wings and a tail – flying high above the cloud-covered mountain peaks.

'Archaeologists say that people have lived in this wonderland of gigantic peaks for a very, very long time, including over a million years of Stone Age man.

Imagine that! The San hunter-gatherers – some people still call them Bushmen – once inhabited the area but all that's left of them now are the thousands of rock paintings to be seen in the many caves.

Unfortunately, the San had disappeared entirely from this mountainous region by the end of the 19th century.

'You won't believe some of the spectacular waterfalls, such as the Tugela Falls, which is one of the highest in the world. Then there's the Amphitheatre and the Giant's Castle and...'

'Ok, Ok ... that's enough, Julia,' said Jessica with a glint in her eyes. 'Let's get on with our fun now!' The group looked around them and saw that the views were stunning and a river flowed directly through the middle of the camp. 'Let's go to the river; we might even see a trout or two,' Jessica added.

The cousins scurried along the path and made their way over to the river. When they arrived, they were astounded to see the rocks covered in what looked like white snow. 'It's snowing,' shouted Jessica and Jarred.

Julia turned and looked at them disdainfully, 'That's not snow, it's frost!'

'How do you know?' asked Jarred, looking at Julia.

'Well, if you look at the mountains you will see they aren't covered in snow and as the river is the coldest part of this valley, frost forms,' she patiently explained to the other two.

'Oh wow, that's cool,' said Jessica.

'We get frost all the time during winter on the farm. Frost is formed when the air temperature drops suddenly and the dew freezes,' Julia imparted to them knowingly.

'How do you know that?' asked Jarred.

Julia just smiled and said, 'My dad teaches me these things.'

The three cousins wandered a little upstream to see if they could see any fish and sent small pebbles skimming across the water. Jarred suddenly shouted and pointed into the water. 'Gold! I have found gold!'

Jessica and Julia ran over to see what he was pointing at, whereupon Jessica screamed, 'We're rich!' and started jumping around on the spot.

Jarred walked up and down the riverbank, flapping his arms like a chicken and chattered, 'Gold! Gold!'

Julia picked up a rock out of the river and pointed at the gold spots embedded in the rock. 'That's not gold, sillies, it's called fool's gold!'

'And I suppose your dad taught you this too?' questioned Jessica. 'It must be gold, look, it shines like gold.'

'No,' laughed Julia, 'my brother Greg taught me about fool's gold. It looks like gold and many years ago people got all excited thinking they had struck it rich, but it actually consists only of iron pyrites, which look like gold. It's quite worthless.'

Both Jarred and Jessica just looked at Julia in horror. They were so disappointed as they had been convinced they had found gold. 'Oh no,' wailed Jessica, 'and here I thought we were going to be rich!'

From the corner of her eye, Julia saw a figure darting back behind a tree. She called out in Zulu, 'Who is there?' and a small, very pretty, black girl ventured hesitantly towards them.

'Sawbona,' said Julia.

'Sunbona,' answered the child.

Jarred and Jessica looked at Julia in awe. 'We didn't know you could speak Zulu, Julia.'

Julia glowed with pride. 'Not many people do. They think just because I live in a white household that I can only speak English, but my dad and Greg speak Zulu fluently and they made sure that I learnt it as well so that I am able to speak to my own people in my mother tongue.'

'Cool,' said Jarred, 'can you teach us?'

'If you like. I just said "hello", that's Sawbona, to this little girl and she greeted me back with Sunbona,' Julia explained.

She then turned to the little girl and asked her in Zulu what her name was, where she came from and where her family home was. The little girl told them that she came from a village a little way up the mountain and her name was Duduzile.

After Julia had translated, Jessica exclaimed what a pretty name it was and the little girl answered her in English saying 'thank you'. Duduzile (or Dudu for short) then explained to them that she went to the local Catholic mission school and English was taught to all the students.

She also told the cousins that she had come down to the river to collect water for her family when had noticed them playing on the banks of the river. She laughed, explaining that the gold Jarred had found was indeed fool's gold, which was plentiful in the surrounding rivers.

The group sat down on the edge of the river bank and chatted happily for a while until they heard the 'clang clang' of the breakfast gong at the camp.

They jumped up, explaining to Dudu that they had to return to camp. Nodding, Dudu said she needed to take the water home for her grandmother to prepare their breakfast as well.

The girls hugged Dudu while Jarred waived and they all agreed to meet again that same afternoon. Dudu promised to show them where to find more fool's gold and all sorts of interesting rocks and paintings in the area. She also told them to bring their costumes along, as there was a place nearby with the most beautiful waterfall and rock pools for swimming.

CHAPTER FIVE

Jessica, Julia and Jarred returned to base camp and made their way to the eating hall. They talked and laughed about the fool's gold, although Jarred was still convinced it must be worth something. Julia tried hard to convince him otherwise, but he was adamant that he was taking some back with him to Cape Town to show his friends.

They spent the rest of the morning in team-building activities such as abseiling. Because it was Jessica's first opportunity to abseil, she was extremely nervous, but both Jarred and Julia shouted encouragement from down below where they had already landed.

After lunch the students were allowed to spend some time exploring the surrounding areas and the group returned to the river bank where they had said goodbye to Dudu. As she was nowhere to be seen, they decided to climb the mountain to find her village.

They discovered a well-used track, which Julia said was probably the way to the village as the villagers obviously used it to collect water from the river. They followed the track for a while and eventually reached a clearing high above the riverbed where the village was situated.

The cousins cautiously ventured into the center of the village, amidst the stares of little children and shouts of greeting from adults. Julia approached one of the adults and asked timidly, in Zulu, where they could find Dudu. The woman pointed in the direction of a large, beautifully decorated reed hut, which was clearly bigger than the others. Julia realised that Dudu's family must be important because they had a larger hut than the rest of the villagers.

As they approached the hut, Dudu ran out and greeted them happily. She took their hands and showed them into the large hut where an elderly man and woman sat around a smoking fire. Dudu very respectfully introduced them first to the old man, her grandfather, whom she called Baba and then to the elderly woman, her grandmother, whom she called Gogo.

The old man welcomed them to his village, then asked Julia why she spoke English so well. When she explained where she came from, they were both shocked and happy to hear her story. The old man said that this was indeed a good time to live in South Africa, where different cultures could live together in harmony. He explained that he was the village chief and Julia, Jessica and Jarred's families were welcome to visit with them at any time in the future because, according to Zulu tradition, their people were now his people.

He laughed when the group told him the story of the fool's gold and said that many years ago his people had also been tricked into thinking this was real gold. Smilingly, he suggested that Jarred should take a small piece back with him to Cape Town to show his people how he very nearly became rich! He then became serious and told them the following story.

'Many years ago, when King Chaka still ruled his people with an iron fist, a boat was shipwrecked off the KwaZulu-Natal Coast. King Chaka sent his Impis (super fit and trained Zulu warriors) down to the beach, as there were very many items that had washed up onto the shore. Amongst these was a gold throne, known as the Peacock Throne.

The king's army spirited this throne away into the mountains where Chaka was lord and master and according to legend, it was still in these mountains. Moreover, the legend says that anyone who touches this throne is cursed and will die before they can reveal its location.'

Julia suddenly became excited. 'I know that story, I know that story. My dad once told me about a man from Ixopo, a farmer, who lived near the Soda Bush. One day one of his staff told him that he had found a great treasure. The farmer was busy at the time and didn't believe in the legend in any case.

He told the worker that he would go and look at it the following day. However, the man said that he needed to go straight away as it was far to travel and if they waited until the next day, he would be dead! He explained that only those who are of the House of Chaka could escape the curse.

The farmer brushed him aside and told him to go away. The following day he wanted the worker to show him the place where he thought he had seen the throne, but the worker had died during the night.

'Yes,' said the chief, 'I know that man, he was my brother!' Jarred and Jessica listened wide-eyed and half in disbelief.

'You mean that the throne really is somewhere in these mountains?' asked Jessica.

'Oh yes,' said the chief, 'but no-one has ever found it again, or if they have, they have not lived to tell the tale.'

Dudu looked at Jarred and Jessica and laughed, 'You guys are so funny! Look at your faces, it's as though you've seen a ghost.'

They all giggled nervously and shyly thanked the chief for his hospitality, but explained that it was time for them to return to their camp. The chief invited them to visit again at any time if they so wished.

As the cousins went down the mountain they remained silent, but when they approached the base Jarred and Jessica burst out laughing and said they were sure Julia and the chief had tricked them.

Julia, who was very serious, said to them, 'I know that story, my dad has told it to us many times before.'

'Are you sure, Julia?' asked Jessica with a glint in her eye.

'Yes, but don't you dare get any ideas! According to the legend, whoever finds the throne will never live to tell the tale and I'm certainly not going to die for the Peacock Throne.'

The group continued down the hillside when Jessica suddenly came to a halt. 'Julia,' she said, her eyes sparkling with excitement, 'didn't you once tell me that your birth surname is of the House of Chaka and, way back, a 100 years' ago, if you had lived in Chaka's time you would have been a princess of the Chaka family?'

'Yes,' said Julia confused. 'My birth surname was Nxumalo, meaning "of Chaka's family".'

'Well, silly,' exclaimed Jessica, 'the curse would not affect you, would it?'

Jarred started jumping about on the spot, once again shouting, 'We're going to be rich, we're going to be rich!'

Wide-eyed, Julia looked at them, slowly starting to smile. 'You are right, the curse would not affect me at all, would it?'

Then suddenly becoming serious, she queried, 'But how will we ever find the Peacock Throne in these mountains, and in what's left of one week?'

Jessica smiled shyly and produced a black leather pouch from around her neck. 'With this.'

'What is that, Jessica?' asked Jarred.

'It's a satellite cell phone with internet access.'

'How on earth is that going to help us?' said Jarred, puzzled.

'Well,' said Jessica, 'we log onto the internet, find a search engine and look up as much information about King Chaka as possible. We then do a search on the origins of the Peacock Throne and find out its density – with that we can plot a possible course that Chaka's impis would have taken into the mountains.

Once we've entered the density, the satellites can search the area plotted and look for a match with an object of the density of the throne.'

The others looked at Jessica in amazement. 'Can you do all that on this small phone?' asked Jarred, clearly bewildered.

'Yes,' said Jessica, 'and not only can I do that on this phone but better still, we can even request the satellites to plot the most likely location.'

'Wait a minute, Jessica,' said Julia, 'I don't know everything about the internet and computers, but I do know that you can't simply tell a satellite what to do and it listens to you. These things cost millions and millions of Dollars and kids like us can't just call up satellites!'

'You are right, but it helps to have friends in high places. When we went overseas two years ago to America, I made a friend of someone, who is into computers and internet in a big way. Ted and I chat online all the time and it just so happens that his father is a scientist for NASA and I am sure we can ask him to help, explained Jessica.

'What is NASA?' asked Jarred.

'NASA stands for the National Aeronautics and Space Administration,' explained Jessica.

'So,' said Jarred, rather disbelievingly, 'you have been chatting online to a NASA scientist's son for two years and now he is just going to arrange access to one of their satellites. Right, pull the other one!'

'No, Jarred, not his dad, I mean Ted. He is one of these brilliant geniuses and often accesses the satellites without anyone's knowledge and plays around. I will ask him to help us out,' said Jessica somewhat importantly.

'Let me get this straight,' said Julia, 'we can use your dad's phone to call a boy in America who can access NASA's billion Dollar satellite for us to find a gold throne? All while we are sitting on an adventure camp in the KwaZulu-Natal Drakensberg... Cool! Way cool!'

She looked first at Jarred who was smiling hugely, then looked at Jessica and said, 'Let's do it, cuz...'

They sat in a cool spot under a tree, while Jessica started typing furiously into her telephone. 'I'm sending him an e-mail now. In America they are online all day and all night – you can do that in South Africa but it's very expensive compared with there. His computer will SMS him if he is not at his workstation, so I hope he will reply soon,' said Jessica.

Sure enough her phone started making small beeping noises and she gleefully said, 'We are in, and talking to Ted.'

She carried on typing for a while, asking questions, answering Ted's and finally shouted, 'Yippee! He's agreed to help and wants to know what he can do. I've asked him to set plans in motion to upload our system to use the satellite and he has already started working on this. I'm going to do a search on the Peacock Throne and King Chaka. We can then plot a possible route the impis took to return to the mountains. After that we can look for a possible density on the throne!' As Jessica continued her search on the internet, Julia and Jarred watched in absolute awe at her abilities. Looking at Jarred, Julia asked, 'How does a ten-year old learn to do this stuff?'

Jessica just laughed, saying, 'Julia, I know computers and you know horses. If I tried to ride a horse I would probably fall off.'

Jarred piped up proudly, 'I can also ride a horse, Julia taught me on the farm.'

Jessica replied, 'All I know about horses is that they have a front and a back and are horribly uncomfortable in the middle. They also pass winds when you ride them. Disgusting!'

They all had a jolly good laugh at this and then sat quietly with their own thoughts whilst Jessica carried on working.

'Right chaps, here it is. This is the history of the Peacock Throne that I researched off the internet from an article in the Sunday Times newspaper:'

PONDOLAND'S DEEP SECRET

More than 200 years after the legendary Grosvenor sank off Transkei's treacherous coast, it continues to offer up new treasures, reports Charles Norman.

A brass plaque raised by divers off the Transkei coast may have solved one of South Africa's most enduring sea mysteries – the location of the three- masted British East Indiaman Grosvenor, which went ashore on the night of August 4, 1782, wrecked by the indecision of a captain who didn't believe until it was too late that his lookouts had spotted coastal grass fires ahead...

The ship certainly carried gold, silver and diamonds, but did she also carry India's fabulous Peacock Throne, owned by Shah Jahan who built the Taj Mahal? The throne was seen in Delhi in the 17th century by the French traveller Jean Baptiste Tavernier, who wrote of the stylised peacocks: 'Their expanded tails were inlaid with sapphires, rubies, emeralds, pearls and other precious stones of approximate colours as to represent life. '

The Legend of the Peacock Throne

Shah Jahan would not have parted with the throne willingly, but India at the time was being well and truly plundered by the British. Only one thing is certain – the Peacock Throne did exist, and it does not exist any more.

It vanished over two centuries ago ... at around the time the Grosvenor sank.

Under an agreement with the previous South African government, a Hungarian syndicate named Octopus has the rights to carry out salvage work at the Bay of Mussels on the Pondoland coast, where the Grosvenor is believed to have sunk. Work here has continued for several years, and chief marine archaeologist Jonathan Sharfman of Cape Town says his team has so far only excavated about 15% of the site ...

Though Sharfman concedes that details of what his team have recovered so far are 'sensitive', many of the items are now on display in the East London Museum. They include navigational instruments, a duelling pistol, a gold pocket watch, brass fittings, and gold and silver coins of the time...

The saga of the Grosvenor and efforts over the years to locate the ship and her passengers is a fascinating segment of early South African history.

On that night 221 years ago, most of the passengers and crew remained on the high poop deck as the ship broke up. The following morning this section tore loose and floated to the shore, with the result that only 15 of her company of 153 drowned.

But the survivors might as well have lost their lives in the surf. Ahead of them stretched a trek down the inhospitable coast to the Dutch settlement at Algoa Bay, and they often had to go far inland to cross major rivers. Three months later only 18 survivors reached Algoa Bay to tell their tale – and start a legend...

Several expeditions were mounted to search for survivors left on the coast during the long walk. The chronicler of one such expedition eight years after the wreck records that the searchers visited a village of yellow-skinned Abelungu, an African tribe of mixed blood who told them that their ancestors were white people who came out of the sea...

Many ships had met their end on this stretch of coast before the Grosvenor did. The Portuguese alone had lost many caravels in the previous two centuries. And long before them, even before Christ, oriental ships had plied the Eastern coast of Africa and almost certainly rounded the Cape; the 'Grosvenor beads' still found along the Pondoland coast after fierce storms are in fact of Indian origin and at least 2 000 years old.

The Legend of the Peacock Throne

*No Grosvenor survivors were found and of a fabulous Indian
throne there was no talk at the time. Almost a century was to pass
before the Grosvenor became a treasure ship. The man most
responsible for this was Captain Sydney Turner, the harbour
master at Port St Johns who – 98 years after the sinking – brought
a mussel-encrusted box containing diamonds and 800 gold coins to
the surface from a depth of 4m.*

*Turner believed he had discovered the wreck of the Grosvenor and
recovered further Indian gold mohurs, Venetian ducats and large
numbers of small gold coins known as star pagodas. But he died
on his third expedition without revealing the location of the wreck
he had found.*

*Was it the Grosvenor? Perhaps, because there certainly was some
wealth on the ship. Coxon is known to have had his life savings of
£8 000 and a box of diamonds with him, and a wealthy passenger
named William Hosea carried diamonds and substantial amounts
of cash in gold and silver coins – India was at that time the
diamond centre of the world; a century before diamonds were
discovered in South Africa.*

*It was around this time, however, that rumours of a larger
treasure began to circulate. As the stories went, the
Grosvenor's official cargo was nothing unusual, but hidden
beneath the silks and spices, lay boxes of jewels ...*

and the fabulous Peacock Throne. Since Turner's discoveries, there have been many attempts to locate and salvage the treasure of the Grosvenor; some of them so bizarre that they were doomed from the start...

Between 1921 and 1926, the Grosvenor Bullion Syndicate attempted to recover the treasure by building a tunnel under the seabed. This venture was denounced as madness by Johannesburg mining engineer E E Beecroft, who had visited the Pondoland coast. His predictions proved correct a few years later when seawater flooded the tunnel. The venture was abandoned...

Beecroft just watched, convinced that all these people were looking in the wrong place...

He would later relate to author Lawrence Green that the magistrate at Umsikaba, some 15 km up the coast from the Bay of Mussels, had showed him a gold ring set with diamonds and sapphires, and told him it came from 'the wreck out in the bay', the bones of which were still visible at low water.

Local residents thought it was the Sao Joao, a Portuguese galleon that had been en route to Lisbon from India when she foundered in the mid-1500s. About 500 survivors reached the shore and set out up the coast to Delagoa Bay in today's Mozambique.

Only eight Portuguese and 17 slaves lived to tell the tale, and the site of the Sao Joao's wreck was never pinpointed.

One calm day, Beecroft rowed out and was able to see that the wreckage was that of only half a ship. He remembered that the Grosvenor had broken in two and wondered if the scattered remains dimly visible beneath him might not be those of the Grosvenor. Local residents were sure they could not be; the Umsikaba relics suggested a small ship, and it was commonly accepted that the Grosvenor had been a huge East Indiaman.

Beecroft's research showed that she had, in fact, been a small ship, whereas the Sao Joao had been a massive galleon... Beecroft submitted pieces of wood from both wrecks for analysis. The sample from the Bay of Mussels was found to be of teak. The Grosvenor was built of stout English oak – and so was Beecroft's wreck at the Umsikaba mouth!

Local native legend gave further strength to Beecroft's belief. Old men who carried the history of their tribe in their heads informed Beecroft that, according to legend, two white men remained at the site of the Umsikaba wreck when the main body of survivors marched away to the south...

But there the Beecroft connection ends. He applied for a permit to search for treasure at the Umsikaba site, intending to 'wash' the entire beach like a diamond area, but his application was refused on the grounds that the rights were held by the syndicate operating at the Bay of Mussels...

Yet in spite of the compelling evidence he compiled for the Umsikaba site, it seems Beecroft had been wrong.

The wreck being excavated by Sharfman's team is indeed at the Bay of Mussels, or at least its northern point – perhaps Beecroft's teak sample came from some other Bay of Mussels wreck, for it is now known there are several in the area.

Sharfman also says the vast number of brass fittings found at the Grosvenor wreck site suggests passengers were bringing furniture back with them; perhaps it was a fragment of teak furniture that Beecroft took for testing. Though the wood analysis remains puzzling, the discovery of the brass plate engraved 'Col Edw James' pretty much confirms that the ship being excavated by Sharfman's team is the Grosvenor.

Yet her mystery endures. Where does the other half of the ship lie, and what cargo did she carry? ...To these questions we will probably never have answers.

The Legend of the Peacock Throne

But as the excavation of the Grosvenor site continues in the years ahead, many other questions about the lost East Indiaman might be answered – including whether the fabulous Peacock Throne lies encrusted with mussels a few metres off a Pondoland beach.

'Wow, this makes absolutely fascinating reading. Just think how the survivors of the Grosvenor must have felt after being shipwrecked on the Transkei Coast. It must have been so scary!' said Jessica. 'So many people have since tried to find this treasure, but no one knows it was actually spirited away by Chaka's impis.'

Look what else I have found on the treasure!' she continued.

Even today the stories continue. From a television program guide for April 2002: 'The British ship Grosvenor, which sank in the Indian Ocean in 1782, may be the final resting place for the crown jewel of the Mogul empire, Shah Jahan's Peacock Throne. Treasure hunters still dive the shark-infested waters looking for it.

A South African publication recently stated that the ship carried the gem-encrusted Peacock Throne of India worth over $10 million; 720 gold ingots worth $2.1 million, 19 chests of diamonds, emeralds, rubies, and sapphires worth $2.6 million; coinage valued at $3.6 million; and millions worth of private treasure carried by passengers or consignments. '

'Gosh … I can't believe it is worth so much!' said Jarred looking at Jessica in awe, not really understanding the treasure's true value. 'We just have to find this amazing treasure,' he said.

'I have figured out the throne's approximate density, which means we can send the information to Ted. Chaka's impis would have followed the old Elephant trail into the mountains and by my calculations we are probably sitting right on top of this trail. I'll send the co-ordinates to Ted and he can start work. We should hear something within a day or two, but it's going to cut it fine as we are only here for the week,' said Jessica.

'I think we should ask Dudu to help as she'll be familiar with the terrain and could possibly point out old caves where the throne may have been hidden. We can start looking in our spare time when we have a break from camp activities,' she continued.

Jarred stood up and stretched, 'All this excitement has made me quite hungry. Let's go back to the camp as it is getting a little darker and becoming rather cold.'

6

CHAPTER SIX

After dinner, the camp organizers took the campers on a game count to identify as many different types of animals as they could. Julia proved to be the best at this exercise as she was used to doing it with her dad on their farm. It's a good conservation practice as landowners can protect their game from poachers and also keep a watch on the natural wildlife, which is a heritage for all.

Jarred fell asleep before they returned to camp and the two girls carried him off to bed. It had been a long and exciting first day for all and they were exhausted.

Early next morning, Jessica woke Julia and Jarred with screams of excitement. 'He's done it! He's done it!'

'What are you talking about, Jessica,' asked Jarred wide eyed and confused at being woken up so suddenly. By his own admission Jarred was not a morning person.

Jessica ran to them with the satellite cell, 'Ted. He's done it!'

Julia jumped across to Jarred's bed where Jessica was showing him the screen on the telephone. 'What's he done, Jessica?'

'He's downloaded possible co-ordinates for our search. He took the information I sent him and used the satellite overnight to track high-density materials in this region; he has four possible locations, all very close by, by the looks of it,' said Jessica.

'Well, let's dress, have our breakfast and start searching. We're lucky to have a free day today and all the time in the world,' suggested Julia.

The three cousins bundled themselves into warm clothing, gobbled their breakfasts and started up the hill. They hadn't progressed very far when Julia hit her head with her hand and exclaimed, 'Oh no, we are stupid! Not very organized treasure hunters are we chaps? No torches, no matches, no first-aid kit, nothing.

We've just rushed out with no planning whatsoever.'

They looked at each another and burst out laughing. Running back to their cabin, they made a note of what was needed for the great treasure hunt!

Jessica set the co-ordinates on her satellite cell and activated the built-in GPS. Jarred grabbed a torch, some candles, a box of matches and the first-aid kit. Julia made up some juice and picked up a packet of biscuits and potato crisps to throw into the backpack. In a more orderly procession they set off up the hill to Dudu's village for some extra help.

After collecting a very bewildered Dudu, the group explained to her what they had in mind.

'You guys are crazy,' she said. 'What about the curse?'

Jarred explained that because Julia belonged to the ancient Chaka clan, the curse did not affect her, only the rest of them, so once they had located the Peacock Throne, it would be up to Julia to retrieve it.

Dudu's face lit up, 'Great, then I can help. I am also a descendent of Chaka, on my mother's side! My mother was related to Chaka's mother, Nandi.'

'So we are almost family,' said Julia, linking her arms with Dudu. Jarred looked at Julia and Dudu, 'Can you perhaps tell me a little more about Chaka and his family?'

Jessica laughed, 'Oh no! Here comes another history lesson.'

Julia looked embarrassed and Jessica felt bad. 'Sorry Julia. I was only teasing. If only I had your knowledge; you must be very proud that you have learnt so much from your dad,' she said.

Julia looked pleased and taking out some notes, she said, 'Well, as I'm descended from Chaka's family, I have done quite a lot of research on this subject.

Briefly, this is what I learnt.'

'The estimated year of Chaka's birth was 1785. He was born to Nandi, daughter of a previous chief of the eLangeni tribe. His father, Senzangakona was the chief of the then small Zulu tribe.

'The marriage of his parents did not last long, and although Nandi returned to her tribe, she was made to feel unwelcome. She then returned to the Zulus, who tolerated her, but they did not treat her well. Chaka was teased and ridiculed and made to feel like an outsider.

'He grew up bitter and angry, hating his tormentors and listening to his mother's tales of his royal blood. Chaka was a young man in his early 20s when he became a warrior for the Mtetwa tribe, fighting for his people. For six years he proved to be an outstanding soldier, believing in being the conqueror, never the conquered. He hated it if another, weaker tribe surrendered before war could take place. He created a dangerous weapon called the "iKlwa".

'Dingiswayo, chief of the Mtetwas, saw Chaka's potential and trained him as a future chief of the Zulus, a tribe conquered by the Mtetwas during Chaka's first battle. Dingiswayo thought that Chaka and the Zulus would act as a buffer against invading forces.

'Chaka rose through the ranks of the Mtetwa army and before long, he became the leader. He carefully and meticulously planned and formatted brilliant battle strategies and altered, where needed, the weapons used during battle.

'When the Zulu chief, Senzangakona died, Chaka became the new chief. The era of Chaka, Zulu king, had started.

'Chaka built up a mighty army of Zulu warriors. He demanded total loyalty and obedience from them. Death was the reward for those who hesitated in carrying out his commands. He drilled his warriors, fine-tuning them into a slick warring machine and devising new battle tactics.

'He lived with his warriors, without the trappings that he was entitled to as chief. Chaka and his warriors, called "impis" were invincible. He believed in total annihilation and only spared those tribes and people who had shown kindness to Nandi, his mother, and the young Chaka.

'After Dingiswayo died the different tribes warred against each other to dominate the Mtetwa empire. Chaka Zulu won the battles and became king of all the territories in the then Natal and southeast region of Africa in 1820.

'White men arrived in Natal in 1824 and sought out Chaka who held them in high regard – they had treated him medically after an attack. In gratitude he signed over land for next to nothing – the Europeans had tricked him, although he was unaware of it.

'When Chaka heard that Nandi was dying, he was demented with grief and ordered that a few thousand people be executed in memory of his mother – a total of 7 000 were slaughtered! He also demanded that his tribe go on a fast to commemorate Nandi and only when many were near to death, did he lift the fast.

'A type of madness seemed to take hold of Chaka and his impis started to lose ground. On 22 September 1828 Chaka, king of the Zulus, was murdered by two half-brothers on his father's side. One of the half-brothers was Dingaan, who immediately claimed kingship.

'Chaka had a mystique about him that lives on. His brilliant battle tactics were revolutionary for those days and his thirst for revenge frightening. He is one of the most famous South Africans ever to have lived.'

Dudu looked at Julia, 'Gosh, you've done your homework on your history. I, unfortunately, know very little about Nandi, Chaka's mother, except that she was a very proud woman who sacrificed a lot for her son.

To this day, the Zulu people use her name "Nandi" to refer to a woman of high esteem.'

'Well, where do we start looking?' she asked, looking very suspiciously at the satellite cell.

'According to the GPS – that's a global positioning system – we should find some sort of a cave about a kilometer and a half from here, in the direction of that mountain,' said Jessica.

'I know that cave well,' said Dudu. 'We used to play in it when we were younger. It has lovely San rock paintings in it and goes very deep into the mountainside. My people told me that this was a sacred cave used for the burial of kings in the past.'

'Jolly dee,' said Jarred in his most posh, fake British accent,

'Tally ho, then off we go to find some treasure!'

The group continued up the hillside in search of buried treasure.

CHAPTER SEVEN

After walking for some time, the children decided to rest under an old tree. They divided the biscuits up amongst themselves and each had a sip of juice. Jessica asked Dudu what she would do with her portion of the treasure if they found it.

Dudu immediately said she would love to build a proper school for her people and hire a few good teachers. Jessica looked at her somewhat puzzled, then asked why they did not have a proper school in the mountains.

'We live so far from the schools in big towns,' she explained, 'and because there are so many children in South Africa, the government is battling to provide proper schools for all, especially in areas that are more difficult to reach.'

Jessica, still a little confused said, 'But I learnt at school that, according to the Constitution of South Africa, it is every child's right to schooling and for those that can't afford it, it is provided free of charge.'

'Yes, Jessica,' Julia said patiently, 'that is the law, but unfortunately the law is not always carried out as it should be.' Thinking about this for a moment, Jessica argued, 'But that's not fair.'

'No it isn't,' agreed Dudu, 'but that's the way it is.' I would also like to build my grandfather and grandmother a brick house and bring my parents back from the cities where they work so we can be a family again.'

By then, Jessica was totally confused, 'What do you mean, "bring your parents back"? Why are they away?'

Dudu smiled at Jessica, 'There are no jobs locally for my parents so they had to travel hundreds of kilometers away to look for employment in the big cities. I only see them once a year at Christmas, as that is the only time they can afford to take off work. They send money home every month to my grandparents, so that we can live.

'My grandfather used to receive an allowance from the government because he is a Chief, but that has been taken away from him and the government no longer pays out this allowance. This has hit us hard and some months we struggle to survive.'

Jarred jumped up and said gruffly, 'Dudu, you can have some of my share so that your family can come home. I know what it is like not seeing your parents. My father lives far away in Pietermaritzburg and I live in Cape Town, so I also only see him once a year and I know what it feels like.'

Julia looked at the group, white and black hugging and sharing their stories and thought to herself quietly that it was good to have friends and family like this.

Jessica piped up and studiously told the group that there was no need to share any portion as, according to her calculations, each portion would be worth millions! All three looked at her with huge eyes. 'What do you mean, worth millions?' asked Julia.

'If you remember, according to the research I did on the Peacock Throne, it was worth $10 million; the 720 gold ingots were worth $2.1 million, 19 chests of diamonds, emeralds, rubies and sapphires were each worth $2.6 million; coinage was valued at $3.6 million, not forgetting the private treasure of passengers and consignments. Keep in mind that we are talking US Dollars here and not South African Rands. With the current exchange rate you can understand why I say millions and millions!'

Jarred sat down suddenly and just stared at Jessica. Julia's mouth formed a big 'O' and Dudu shook her head in disbelief. 'That's hundreds of millions, Jessica! Wow!' said Julia.

Jarred jumped up and started his jiggly dance again, chanting, 'We're rich, we're rich!'

Dudu gave herself a huge hug, while Jessica grinned like a Cheshire cat and they all burst out laughing.

'Let's not count our chickens,' Jessica warned, 'let's get this treasure hunt under way.' They all stood up and continued their long walk up the mountainside.

CHAPTER EIGHT

Yuck!' screamed Jessica, 'You didn't tell me there'd be spiders.' They had found the first cave and were cautiously making their way down a long tunnel.

'Yup,' said Julia, 'and there are probably snakes in here too.'

Dudu laughed at them and told them the snakes were probably more scared of them than they should be of the snakes. 'Remember, as you walk your feet give off vibrations that the snakes sense and, unless we come across a nest, we're quite safe,' she warned.

Suddenly Julia's torch picked up something drawn on the walls of the cave. Beautiful, colourful, stick-like drawings showing images of what appeared to be a hunting scene.

Dudu explained to the others that these caves had once been the home of a group of San people. The San were known as the Bushmen in years gone by.

Unfortunately, this quiet, gentle nation had been wiped out by both the settlers and Chaka's tribes alike, and forced either into slavery by Chaka's impis or hunted down like prey by the settlers.

Jarred shook his head in disgust, 'Why do people do things like this? It's disgusting!'

They carried on their hunt and eventually came to a dead end. There was no more to be seen in this cave. Looking despondent, they started to make their way back to the entrance while Jessica tried to cheer them up. 'Don't worry,' she said, 'we have three more sites to go.'

Back in the open air, Jessica again activated the GPS. She suggested that they should travel in an easterly direction for about two kilometres, then climb a further 500 m up the mountain. It was a lovely walk in the open hillside and the children chatted as they walked along the numerous paths that criss- crossed the mountainside. The air was fresh and clean, and the sky an azure blue they had never seen before.

Dudu pointed out interesting landmarks along the way, explaining what the different plants were and what they were used for in herbal healing ceremonies. She showed them a plant called imfino, which was cooked in a similar way to spinach and eaten as a vegetable by the people of her tribe. She said it was extremely tasty as well as healthy. She showed them where a group of wild pigs had dug up the ground looking for root plants, and where the duiker had eaten the tasty, sweet, new leaves off some nearby bushes.

She also pointed to a small bird, called a bee eater, and told them if they had the time to follow it, it would most surely lead them to a bee hive nearby. It was African tradition to follow such a bird, retrieve the honey, then place the choicest piece of honeycomb for the bee eater to eat, thereby ensuring that both humans and the bird benefited.

Jarred turned to Dudu in admiration, 'Dudu, you are like a walking wildlife encyclopedia!'

Dudu simply laughed, explaining that all children growing up in Africa should learn the basic lessons of nature to live in harmony with animals and plants.

She said, 'My grandfather has taught me many things but one of the most important of all is that red is the colour of danger!

My father took me into the bush at an early age and taught me to recognize poisonous plants and insects. The majority of these are almost always red or very bright in colour. It is nature's way of sending a warning to say "Watch out! I am not to be eaten!"'

After walking for approximately an hour, they reached what appeared to be a dead end. The rock face was solid and there were no signs of any caves in the area. All four looked at one another in bewilderment.

'What now?' asked Jarred, kicking at a rock.

'I don't know,' said Jessica. 'My GPS is still working and it tells me there should be a cave here but I don't see it.'

They walked around aimlessly for a while, then decided not to waste time but to go on to the next site, which according to their calculations was not too far away. After another 30 minutes they found another cave, similar to the first they had explored and went inside.

Dudu immediately stiffened and shouted, 'Stop!'

The others stopped dead in their tracks and turned to her enquiringly. 'What's wrong, Dudu?' asked Julia.

'Don't you smell it?' she said.

'Smell what?' said Jarred.

Julia took a few sniffs in the stale air, 'Yes, you are right. I can smell it. Don't move anyone!'

Looking perplexed, Jarred asked, 'Smell what? What are you two playing at?'

Jessica looked at both Dudu and Julia and said seriously, 'What is it girls? What are we smelling?

It smells sweet to me.'

'Exactly!' exclaimed Dudu. 'That sweet smell means snakes, lots and lots of snakes. This cave is obviously used as a snake nest, very dangerous snakes at that.'

'The Berg is full of very dangerous snakes,' said Julia. Look at this snakeskin lying on the floor – this is a particularly nasty one, the diamond back puff adder. A bite from one of these beauties and you'll be in serious trouble. We would never get back to camp in time for an anti-venom injection, so you would simply die on the mountain!'

'Julia is right,' said Dudu, 'a while back one of the herd boys herding cattle was bitten by this type of snake and he was dead before nightfall,' she said.

'Oh boy,' said Jarred, 'first spiders, now venomous snakes, what are we doing?'

'Just walk slowly back towards the entrance, Jarred, and you will be fine,' said Julia.

The children slowly and carefully made their way back to the entrance and stepped out into the fresh air and bright sunshine. 'Now what do we do?' asked Jarred. 'We can't search a cave full of rattlers, can we now?'

Julia laughed, 'Jarred, you watch far too many cowboy movies. They aren't rattlers. That's American. You won't find any rattlers here in South Africa!'

Jessica looked pensive for a moment and checked the time on her watch. 'It's 2.30 already and we don't have time to search any longer. I also don't like the look of those clouds over there, they look pretty dark.'

'Yes,' agreed Dudu, 'we're going to have one our famous Berg storms. I also think we should head back.'

The group started its long trip back to the village and before long the rain started coming down – large droplets that stung like mad. Jarred immediately ran for cover under a tree, but Dudu rushed up to him and pulled him away.

'Hey, what are you doing, Dudu?' he asked, alarmed.

'Never, ever take shelter under a tree in a storm,' she told Jarred, who looked at her bewilderedly.

'Why?' he asked.

'Should there be lightning, the first place it will strike is the highest point,' she explained, 'and in this case the highest point around is that tree.'

'Oh, thanks Dudu, I would never have known that,' said Jarred.

They ran down the mountainside, wetter and wetter with every step and finally arrived in the village where they ran for cover into the big hut.

Before very long, the storm had passed and they had dried themselves with towels from Dudu's grandmother who had made them strong, black cups of tea sweetened with lots of sugar. They agreed to meet again after breakfast the following day and Julia, Jarred and Jessica made their way back to camp.

CHAPTER NINE

During the night, Jessica woke up in a panic shouting, 'Snake! Snake!' Jarred and Julia found it quite difficult to calm her down because she said her nightmare had been so real that she had been very scared.

All three looked at one another and suddenly realized how much real danger they had been in, inside the snakes' cave. If it hadn't been for Dudu, they would have marched into danger without a thought. They promised one another they would be far more careful the following day.

Jarred sat quietly on the bed for some time, then asked, 'But what if the snakes' cave is the cave with the treasure?' All three looked horrified.

'Well I certainly am not going into any snake-infested cave for anyone, not even for 20 million!' said Julia.

Jessica pointed out that there was only one more place to search the following day and that would be it.

'But what about the place we went to today, where we found no cave?' asked Julia. 'Do you think it may be buried?'

'I don't know,' answered Jessica, 'the GPS was very specific. There should have been a cave there.'

'Well, said Julia, 'why don't we go to the last location on the GPS and if there is nothing in that cave, we head back to the missing cave area?'

All three agreed and decided to get plenty of rest before they continued the adventure the following day.

CHAPTER TEN

This cave looks just like the first one,' remarked Jarred, looking around at the San paintings on the wall.

'Spiders too!' observed Julia. She wondered over to a painting on the far side and excitedly called to the others, 'Come and look at this painting, it has a picture of the throne in it, or what looks as though it could be a throne.'

The other three rushed over to where Julia was standing and all had a long, hard look at the painting. 'Look, there's the cave entrance, and what looks like a mountain between this cave and the throne,' Julia said.

Jessica studied the painting for a while further and turned to the others. 'According to these paintings, the throne doesn't appear to be in this cave – it's either in the snake-infested cave or the cave that's not there.'

The children looked at one another in bewilderment. What were they going to do?

'I have an idea,' said Julia. 'I'll give my brother, Greg, a call and explain about the snakes, he'll know what to do.'

'Good idea, Julia, but don't you think if you make that call to your brother and tell him that you want to go into a cave infested with puff adders, he'll probably tell your parents?' asked Jarred, looking concerned.

'Hmm, you could be right, Jarred. But what else can we do?' asked Julia.

'I know, let's return to the site where the cave is supposed to be – but isn't – then we can hunt around to see what we come up with,' suggested Jessica.

They all agreed and set off to find the cave that didn't exist. After a while of poking around in bushes and clambering about on rocks at the site of the non-existent cave, they sat down looking really dejected.

'I really just don't know what to do! The GPS says it's here, but it's not! What now? I certainly don't want to brave puff adders! The treasure hunt isn't as easy as I thought it would be,' Jessica said, disappointed.

Dudu, who had been quiet for some time, stood up and walked over to the cliff face. She picked up a stick and prodded it into the vines, gave up and sat down again. They all sat staring at the rock face for a while, at a loss as to what to do. Suddenly, out of nowhere, they heard baboons barking.

Jarred jumped up, shouting 'What's that?'

Jessica ran around asking 'What do we do?' while Julia looked horrified and Dudu sat extremely still.

'Shoo!' she whispered to the others. 'Sit here next to me and keep extremely quiet. Don't dare move a muscle!' The others clambered up onto the rock where she sat, some distance from the rock face and joined her there.

'Where are they?' asked Jarred. 'I can't see them but they sound as though they're right next to us.'

'Shoo,' said Dudu, 'watch!' The next moment the cliff face erupted with moving bodies as a troop of baboons appeared as if from nowhere and jumped to the bottom of the cliff. The baboons paid no attention to the group and ran off into the distance, barking and shouting to one another.

Dudu stood up and squealed, 'There it is! There's our cave!' She pointed up to where the baboons had appeared out of the rocks.

'But how do we get up there?' wailed Jessica. 'I'm scared of heights and can't climb to save my aunty!' she added, looking down at her designer bling takkies with a lovely wedge heel.

'It's easy,' said Julia, 'look how the vines are growing. All we have to do is climb up these vines like a stepladder.'

Jarred took Jessica's hand and showed her how to climb up the rock face. She battled a little, but finally managed to reach the entrance that Dudu had made by pulling back the vines. The four cautiously made their way into the cave, fearing an onslaught of more baboons, but all was quiet inside.

'This is the perfect cave to hide any treasure,' exclaimed Julia. 'You can't see it from the outside and it looks as though it's been hidden for hundreds of years!'

Dudu looked around, 'This is the type of cave they used to bury my ancestors in. This is definitely a cave fit for a king!'

Jessica spun around with a frightened-looking face, 'Do you think this is a burial cave, Dudu?' she asked, now scared out of her wits.

'Maybe,' said Dudu, 'but what better place to hide a treasure? The locals would not come near here for fear of the dead, so the treasure would be perfectly safe.'

Julia looked around and excitedly tapped Jessica on the arm, 'Do you know what I think, Jessica, I think we are here!'

Jessica also looked around and her face broke out into a huge grin. Imitating Jarred's posh English accent, she said, 'Precisely dear Watson, precisely! Let's do it guys, off we go, tally ho.'

Still nervous, the children slowly made their way into the dark and dingy cave. Again they found San drawings on the walls, but these were more serious than the previous ones, showing small people being hunted like wild animals by larger stick figures – some white, some dark. 'This is part of the history of the San people. We'd heard that it had been recorded but didn't know if anyone had ever seen such drawings before. This is definitely a sacred cave,' said Dudu.

Cautiously, the children followed a route along the length of the cave until their path reached a fork. 'What should we do now?' asked Jarred.

Julia suggested they split up but both Jarred and Jessica shouted there was no way they were going on alone. The four decided to take the right fork and see where it led them.

They walked for a short distance and came to what looked like a small chamber. In the center of the chamber they saw a sight which none of them would forget for the rest of their lives...

CHAPTER 11

In the center of the room sat what appeared to be a figure leaning over. The group stared in horror. Surrounded by dozens of earthenware pots, the figure was draped in robes of animal skins that resembled a shroud. The torchlight just picked up glints from the pots and small, carved figures in the shapes of wild animals were also dotted around the pots.

Dudu looked at this sight reverently and her mouth formed the shape of an 'O'. 'I can't believe it!' she exclaimed. She really looked incredibly shocked. The others looked at her in confusion.

'What is it, Dudu?' asked Julia.

'Julia, it's a burial chamber. I have heard about these in stories told by the old people of the tribe, but never in my life did I think I would see one,' she said, shaking her head. 'Only the most important people were buried in this manner. So this person must either have been an extremely important chief of the Royal House of Chaka or part of Chaka's family,' she explained.

'Do you mean,' said Jarred, 'that we are looking at dead royalty here! Cool.'

Julia turned and made a face at Jarred, 'Be quiet Jarred! This is an important discovery we have made. It's also very important for the Zulu nation. Here lies one of their own. Buried secretly all those years ago. Besides the person here, there will also be important artifacts of great cultural worth.'

Jessica walked up to the lone figure and peered closely at it. 'I can't tell if it's a man or a woman,' she said. 'The skin has dried over the face like a mummy. Look here, look at these pots. They're filled to the brim with what looks like coloured, shiny stones. There are red and green ones and these white ones look very much like diamonds to me. Oh my gosh! You had better come and see this. Yellow stones, which, if I am not mistaken, are gold nuggets!'

The others rushed to the spot where Jessica stood and peered closely into the pots. There were 12 pots placed around the shrouded figure, together with the carved animals and what looked like cooking utensils and cooking pots.

Dudu walked slowly around the figure and told the others that it was Zulu custom to bury the very important dead with their personal wealth and articles they would need for the afterlife – very much like the traditions of the ancient Egyptians.

However, she had never heard of such wealth being placed with a person. This indeed must have been a very, very important person.

'Do you think this could be Chaka Zulu?' piped up Jarred, looking very pleased with himself.

Dudu laughed, 'No, his burial place is located on the KwaZulu-Natal North Coast in a town formerly known as Stanger, now called KwaDukuza.'

Dudu quietly walked around the figure once more. As she looked up, her eyes became suddenly bright. 'Do you know, they have never located Chaka's mothers grave and as far as I am aware she, Nandi, was from these parts. My mother's family is closely related to her – that's why we are of the House of Chaka,' she explained.

Julia looked at Dudu with huge eyes, 'Dudu, do you have any idea what this could mean for you and your tribe? You will suddenly be catapulted into the spotlight and this whole area will be declared a national heritage site. Your village will be on the map and become a tourist destination!'

Dudu looked at Julia with equally large eyes. 'Yes, you are right! This could certainly change things. The government would then notice our tribe and it might even possibly be forced to build schools, upgrade our roads and provide proper housing for my people,' she exclaimed.

She hugged herself and did a little dance around the cave. 'This is going to be so good for our people – if it is Nandi,' she said.

'Ok,' said Jessica, 'I hate to break up the party, but we still haven't found the Peacock Throne! It certainly isn't here. These jewels and artifacts belong to the Zulu nation, so we are certainly not going to get rich on these. Do you think we should head back and try the other tunnel?' she asked.

'Yes! Yes!' shouted Jarred, 'I want my millions.'

Julia looked up from the shrouded figure and looked at her watch. 'We can't do any more today, look at the time. We should have been back at camp two hours ago. We are in big trouble!'

The children ran down the tunnel in the cave. They looked longingly at the entrance to the other tunnel and finally made their way out the caves and down the side of the cliff.

CHAPTER 12

When Jessica, Julia and Jarred finally returned to the camp it was almost dark. They knew immediately they were in huge trouble and instead of trying to sneak back into their room they decided to face their camp leaders with a plausible reason why they had been missing from camp for five hours.

Starting down the path to the camp headquarters, Jessica tripped and hurt her ankle. It wasn't too bad and she managed to stand on it after a few minutes, but her ankle had swelled up and it certainly looked worse than it felt. Jarred and Julia looked at Jessica, then at each other and both made a dive for the first aid kit lying on the floor where Jessica had dropped it when she fell.

After some furious activity, Jessica's ankle was impressively bound up in record time and both cousins were looking very pleased with themselves. Jessica, still not too sure what was happening, looked at them in disgust, 'What was that for? It's only a sore ankle, I haven't broken it you know.'

Julia looked at Jessica with a glint in her eye, 'Oh, but Jessica, it is very bad! Can't you see how swollen it is?'

'Yes,' agreed Jarred, 'you are so lucky you did not break it you know. Falling down that cliff face was a horrible experience and we could have lost you!

As it was, it took us nearly four hours to carry you back to base camp.'

Jessica looked at Julia then at Jarred, who by then was grinning broadly. She said, 'You two have gone mad. You've now lost it completely. What are you talking about, four hours back to base camp? I just fell now and hurt my ankle, I never fell off any cliff!'

As she uttered the last word, suddenly she understood perfectly what the other two were driving at – they would have to face their camp leaders and were in real trouble. But this just might save the day. She smiled and took a very exaggerated step forward. 'Oh no! I can't stand the pain. You two will simply have to carry me in,' she said with a wicked grin.

Julia and Jarred crossed hands allowing Jessica to jump onto them, then they unceremoniously they carried her the last 50 meters into the camp amidst great groans of what sounded like real pain uttered by her.

A few hours later, once the cousins had completed their dinner and after Jessica had been fussed over and all had heard the horrific story of how she very nearly lost her life falling down a cliff face, the children settled in their cabin feeling rather pleased with themselves.

Julia looked up at Jessica and giggled, 'You can stop groaning now, Jessica! No-one is here to hear you.'

'Hmm... all this groaning and moaning is making me tired, although I must admit I do feel a little bit guilty for telling this very exaggerated fib.'

Julia looked up from some papers she had been studying, 'Yes, Jessica, so do I, but remember if we had not had a good excuse we probably would have been punished. Then we wouldn't be able to find the Peacock Throne at all.' All three of them looked serious at the thought.

The following morning, Jarred and Julia volunteered to look after Jessica all day at camp while the rest of the children and their team leaders headed off to spend the day visiting the Drakensberg Boys' Choir. They would also be having a late lunch there and were only expected back at around 5:30 pm. This gave the three cousins ample time to go back up into the mountains, find Dudu and continue their search for the missing Peacock Throne!

CHAPTER 13

Julia, Jessica and Jarred almost ran up the mountainside early that morning to meet up with Dudu. They were all so excited because they were sure that that was the day they would become millionaires.

Fortunately, Jessica had worn sensible takkies that morning and her ankle had definitely mended. The climb up into the cave was quick and orderly. Once the group was inside, torches were quickly switched on and the children made their way into the tunnel they had been unable to explore the previous day.

They were almost half way down the tunnel when they suddenly reached a wall of rocks packed up all the way to the tunnel roof.

'Oh no!' wailed Jessica. 'Look at these rocks, how are we ever going to move them?'

Julia walked up to the stacked rocks and said, 'These look as though they've been here for years.

There must have been a rock fall some time ago and now the entrance to the cave is blocked, or maybe it was done deliberately so that no one would find the hidden treasure, or even suspect that there was anything to be found.'

Jarred sat down on a large rock that had rolled down to the side of the tunnel and stared.

The four walked round in circles and surveyed the absolute mess of rocks. Eventually, Julia turned to Jessica and said, 'Right, I know when we are beaten. It's time to call in reinforcements!'

Jessica looked at her and nodded in agreement while Jarred jumped up. 'But who can we trust with our great secret, Julia? If we call in any strangers now we will lose our great treasure,' he said sadly.

Julia simply smiled and looked at Jarred. 'Jarred, who in our family is almost as bad as us when it comes to adventure?' she asked with a huge grin.

Jarred looked at her for a moment then smiled, 'Right, I get it. I know who you want to call in to help us.'

Dudu looked at the three who all had huge smiles on their faces. She asked, 'Who do you want to call?'

Julia came over to her and said, 'Dudu, don't look so worried. We're going to contact Greg, my brother. He is probably worse than we are when it comes to sniffing out an adventure. Who do you think taught us all the ropes?'

'How long do you think it will take for him to get here?' asked Jarred, wondering aloud.

'Well, it just so happens that Greg is here in the Berg with his friends,' said Julia. 'He is having one last holiday with them before he leaves for Cape Town to study at the university. He's probably only about an hour away.'

The group made its way out of the tunnel again and back down the cliff face. Julia took Jessica's phone and started dialing her brother Greg's number.

'Greg, is that you?' she said into the phone.

'Yes, Julia, what's up?' asked Greg. 'Are you chaps in trouble again?

I had a feeling I was going to hear from you.'

'Are you doing anything important at the moment?' Julia asked him mysteriously.

'No,' he said, 'we're just relaxing at the pool.'

'Do you think you and your mates could spare a couple of hours?' continued Julia, still giving no explanation.

'Well,' said Greg, 'we could come over to your camp, but what's the problem? You're being very secretive over the phone.'

'I can't explain now,' said Julia, 'but we need as many strong men as we can find at the moment and we also need people you can trust.'

Greg thought about this for a moment. 'Right, we'll come now but you had better have a very good reason for disturbing our relaxing day,' he said sounding stern, but with a wide smile creasing his face.

'We definitely have,' she answered, 'but don't go to the camp as we aren't there. Take the road just before the camp, which leads you up to a village on the mountainside. We've asked a friend of Dudu's, a young boy by the name of Sipho, to meet you there. He'll show you where we are and we'll be waiting about a half hour's walk from the village.'

'This all sounds very mysterious, Julia,' said Greg. 'I hope you're not in trouble again!'

'No, Greg, we are fine, but we really need you to get here as a matter of urgency,' Julia said emphatically.

CHAPTER 14

The four friends decided to have something to eat and drink whilst they waited for Greg and his friends to arrive. They opened their snack boxes and spread a small cloth on the ground so that they could share one another's food.

Jarred looked at Dudu's box and exclaimed, 'Dudu, what's that white stuff in your lunch box?'

Dudu and Julia laughed and Dudu said, 'It's phutu, Jarred, have you never eaten phutu?'

'No,' he said, 'I have never seen that in my life, what is it?'

Julia explained, 'Phutu is made from maize, Jarred. It's cooked

over a slow heat until it swells up and is either eaten with a tomato and onion gravy, or with sugar and milk as porridge. It's the staple food of most black people in South Africa and is very good for you.'

Jarred looked at the phutu and asked Dudu shyly, 'Do you think I could try some, Dudu?'

'Of course, Jarred… here have a bit. Roll it up into a little ball and eat it with your meat.'

Jarred rolled some phutu into a little ball and popped it into his mouth with a little meat and chewed for a while. 'It's delicious,' he declared. 'I'm going to ask my mum to make some for us when we get back to Cape Town.' All four laughed and then sat eating quietly, absorbed with their own thoughts of what lay beyond those rocks in the cave.

'Look!' shouted Julia. 'Here comes Sipho, as well as Greg and his friends.' The four jumped up and ran down the hillside to where Sipho, Greg and his four mates were climbing up the hillside.

'Greg,' called Julia, 'we are over here.'

Greg walked up to the group. 'Ok, monkey, what are you up to up here in the mountains?' he asked in a mock stern voice.

Dudu looked a bit worried for a moment and looked at Julia. Julia laughed and gave Greg a big hug. 'Greg, best you sit down here... we need to tell you a story,' she said gravely.

'In a moment', he said, 'first I'd like you to meet my friends. This is Craig, Thomas, Brett and Garth.'

Once all the introductions had been completed, Julia sat down with Greg and looked him squarely in the face. 'Do you remember the story Dad told us about the farmer whose worker came to him in Ixopo and said he had found the Peacock Throne in the Soda Bush?'

Greg's head snapped up and he looked at her with wide eyes. 'Don't tell me you've found the Peacock Throne, Julia,' he said, looking highly alarmed. 'I always assumed that was just a story Dad used to tell in the pub to keep people amused. I should have known better.'

Becoming pensive Greg continued, 'Do you remember what happened last time with one of the stories he told you and how you chaps proved it was true.

That was one adventure of yours that I still can't believe happened. I think you'd better tell me everything.' Looking suddenly worried, he said, 'Don't forget that there's a curse attached to this story and remember also what was supposed to have happened to the worker who claimed he had found the Peacock Throne!'

Julia and Greg sat quietly to one side whilst Julia related exactly what had happened and what they had found in the hidden caves so far. She also explained the part about the rocks and why they needed help from the young adults.

Greg listened to her tale, then said, 'You're telling me that some kid in the USA has used a NASA satellite to help you track this cave! You've also found a long-dead person of the Zulu royal family who has pots of jewels around him or her and now you want us to help you move some rocks so that you can claim the Peacock Throne, which you say must be in a cave behind those rocks. This is unbelievable!'

'I know,' smiled Julia.

Greg looked at his sister in awe and then said seriously, 'But what about the curse? If this story is true then there is a real threat that this cave is indeed cursed and cannot be opened.'

Julia smiled broadly and brought Dudu over to where they were sitting, 'Greg, meet Dudu.'

Greg greeted Dudu respectfully in Zulu and she explained to him that she was a direct descendent of Chaka's family on her mother's side. She waited before she added, 'And so is Julia!'

At that Greg looked slightly startled. 'Of course,' he said aloud, 'you are indeed a direct descendent as well because of your birth surname!' He added smilingly, 'We forget that you are adopted, Julia. We are all one family and I never think about the fact that you are adopted.'

Greg thought for a while then stood up. 'Ok chaps,' he said to his friends, 'I hope you're all feeling strong. My sister needs our help – we're going on a real African Treasure hunt!'

After a flurry of excited questions and conversation, Julia showed them the way to the cave entrance. They trooped in and made their way towards the area where the rocks had fallen and blocked the cave entrance.

It was heavy, sweaty work but bit by bit the tunnel entrance was revealed to them. They had dug away at the rocks for over two hours and were eventually able to see beyond the rocks into the tunnel itself. Once the hole was large enough for all of them to fit through, the treasure hunters bravely set off down the tunnel in search of the cave.

CHAPTER 15

After walking for some while, they reached a sharp curve in the tunnel. Turning the corner, they suddenly found themselves in the cave. Stunned at the sight before them, they stopped dead in their tracks. It was at least five minutes before anyone ventured a word.

The Legend of the Peacock Throne

Greg walked slowly forwards, then whispered, 'Holy moly! I don't believe what I am seeing!'

Julia followed him and laid a restraining hand on his shoulder before he could touch anything. 'Stop, Greg! Remember the curse,' she warned. With that, Greg rapidly backed off and stood at a distance, trying to take it in.

They had found the treasure and what a treasure it was! Before them, standing on a raised stone platform was the Indian Peacock Throne in all its splendor. Scattered around the throne were sea chests filled with what appeared to be shiny gold nuggets. No-one in that room had never seen such a sight.

Julia turned, took Dudu's arm and together they walked forward to lay the first hands on the Peacock Throne, which had been lying there for hundreds of years.

The throne was magnificent! Its blue and green jewels sparkled in the torchlight, almost life-like. Together Julia and Dudu tried to move the throne, but it wouldn't budge. The solid gold throne was backed by figures of two peacocks, their beautiful colours created by countless inlaid precious stones.

Between them was the figure of a parrot carved out of a single, massive emerald.

The weight of the throne was such that it would require more than the strength of five young men to carry it. Julia managed to lift some of the gold bars and took them for the others to see. She handed one each to Jessica, Dudu and Jarred. The four raised their bars above their heads and squealed with joy. They had found their treasure and it was magnificent!

By that stage, Greg and his friends were able to touch the throne as both Julia and Dudu had broken the power of the curse by touching it first.

With much huffing and puffing, they shifted it off the platform onto the ground. They also moved the solid sea chests filled with gold ingots.

Greg turned to the rest of them, 'We're going to need much more help to move this from the cave.'

Dudu looked up from where she stood, 'My grandfather is in the village, we must tell him what we've found. He and our villagers are honest people. They'll give us all the help we need.'

Greg agreed with Dudu and proposed that he and Dudu make their way back to the village with little Sipho and request help from her family. He also suggested that he contact his father, as they would need advice from people who understood the importance of their find. It was also important that the cousins' find should be credited to them and that they, in fact, benefited from this. He asked Dudu where her father might be contacted in Durban as he thought it would be a good idea if his own father collected her father on the way up to the Berg.

Greg, Sipho and Dudu made their way out the cave and back through the tunnel into the fresh air. They returned to the village and proceeded to explain to both Dudu's grandfather, the chief, and grandmother about the great historical find they had made in the mountains.

Greg also rang his father, who promised that he would find the relevant help and be there within four hours. With any luck, the head of the archaeological society based at the University of KwaZulu-Natal, who happened to be a friend of his, and Dudu's father would accompany him.

CHAPTER 16

Julia, Jessica, Jarred and Dudu sat around the campfire chatting quietly, whilst the adults made various plans for the future of the treasure. The four of them couldn't believe how
much activity had taken place since they had found the treasure that morning.

Dudu's grandfather had arrived with help from the village and the caves had been secured with guards until help arrived from Julia's father – in the form of the head of the Archaeological Society of KwaZulu-Natal. Both the burial cave and the treasure cave had been photographed and mapped out before anything was moved. Julia's dad had registered the children's claim to the treasure and at the same time had registered the villagers claim to the burial site. Government officials had swarmed all over the place and both the Peacock Throne and treasure from the cave, as well as the contents of the burial site had been loaded up and taken away to a place of safety.

Julia's dad walked across to the four to find out how they were doing. He said, 'I'm very proud of you chaps! What you found here today will go down in the history of this country. Well done.' Julia turned to her father shyly, 'Dad, if you hadn't told us this story we would never have found the treasure. It's because you used to tell us all these adventure stories that we have managed to make another great discovery!'
Her father looked at her fondly, 'I'm a great believer in reading books and learning about our history, Julia, you know that, and it's because of this that both you and Greg, and hopefully Morag, will continue to believe in the unbelievable.'
He turned and walked away and the children continued to chat amongst themselves. Jessica looked up eventually, 'I can't believe this is all over, what will we do now? The rest of the holiday is going to be an anticlimax after all this excitement.'

They sat quietly for a while, thinking about this, when suddenly Jarred looked up at Julia and with a huge grin he said, 'So tell me, Julia, what other stories has your dad told you recently and where are we going on holiday next July?'

Julia giggled at the three gathered around her, 'Well, there are a few other stories… such as the English farmer in Ixopo who jumped onto his horse whenever it was misty and rode out into his fields blowing his hunting bugle. People whispered that he was not all there and one day he never returned.

Then again, I haven't told you the story of Kruger's Gold, have I?'

www.ingramcontent.com/pod-product-compliance
Lightning Source LLC
Chambersburg PA
CBHW071336130626
46556CB00004B/1922